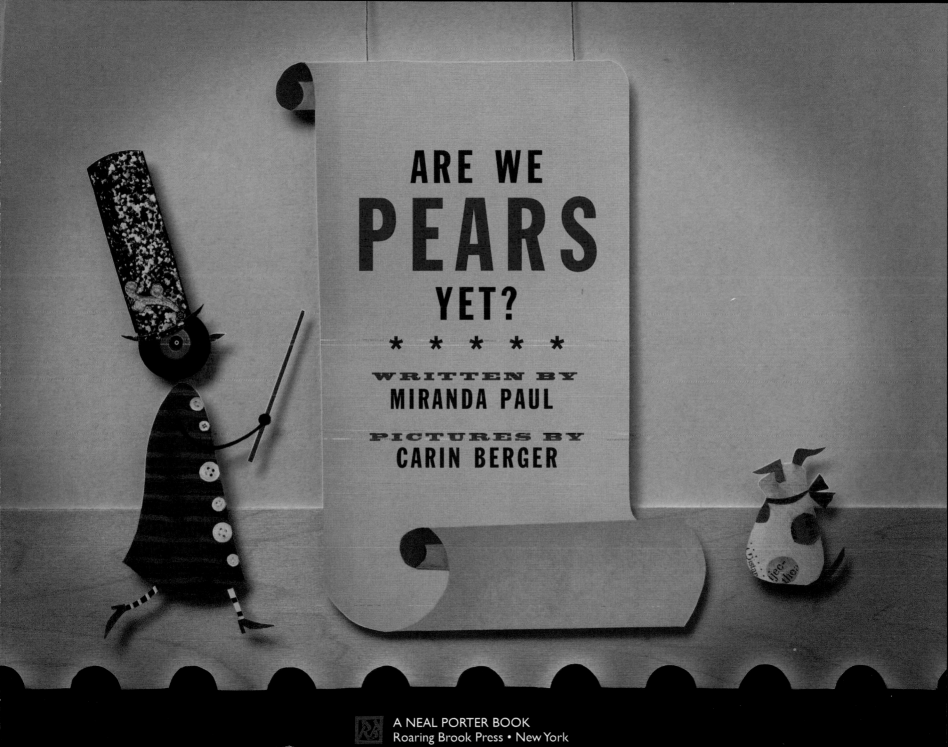

ARE WE
PEARS
YET?

* * * * *

WRITTEN BY
MIRANDA PAUL

PICTURES BY
CARIN BERGER

A NEAL PORTER BOOK
Roaring Brook Press • New York

For my drama club friends,
especially Sarah Doyle and April Deming
—M.P.

To Alice, Lisa, and Pearly
with love and gratitude
—C.B.

Photography by Porter Gillespie

Text copyright © 2017 by Miranda Paul
Illustrations copyright © 2017 by Carin Berger
A Neal Porter Book
Published by Roaring Brook Press
Roaring Brook Press is a division of Holtzbrinck Publishing Holdings Limited Partnership
175 Fifth Avenue, New York, NY 10010
mackids.com
All rights reserved

Cataloging-in-Publication Data is on file at the Library of Congress
ISBN: 978-1-62672-351-1

Our books may be purchased in bulk for promotional, educational, or business use.
Please contact your local bookseller or the Macmillan Corporate and Premium Sales
Department at (800) 221-7945 ext. 5442 or by e-mail at
MacmillanSpecialMarkets@macmillan.com.

First edition 2017
Book design by Carin Berger
Printed in China by RR Donnelley Asia Printing Solutions Ltd.,
Dongguan City, Guangdong Province

1   3   5   7   9   10   8   6   4   2

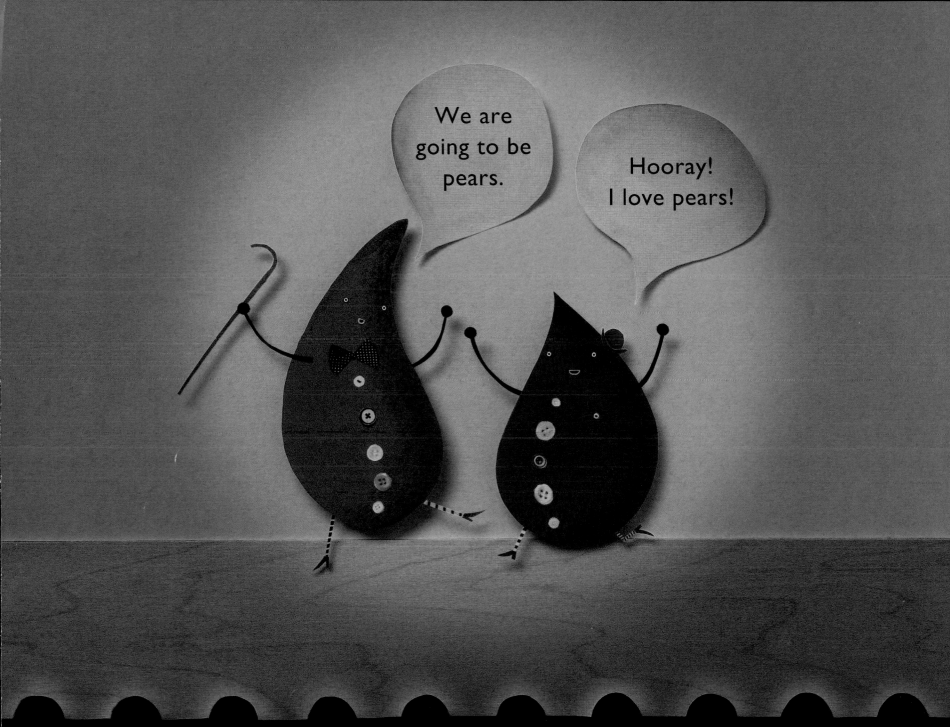

HOORAY, SUN!

2 YEARS LATER

Z Z Z Z Z Z Z Z Z Z Z

ONE
YEAR
LATER

X·RAY

I love theater, because stage plays introduce us to characters who grow and change. Sometimes, I feel that our world is one giant theater, and nature is my favorite stage. Science knows how to put on a good show, and fruit trees are incredible "characters" to watch—they start out small and fragile, grow and blossom, and provide animals and people with nutrients and delicious ingredients that make us feel cozy and happy.

When this book idea first popped in my head, I thought it was a little ridiculous. But in my research I discovered many ways in which pears and people are similar, and I became fascinated with the idea of giving these seeds a life of their own. Real pear trees need certain conditions to live—just as humans do. Pears need soil, water, sunlight, and a cold period. Pear trees also need other pear trees (as well as pollinators) if they want to reproduce—which is like saying they have to make "friends" in order to survive. If you plant pear seeds, the pears you'll eventually get will be different than the ones they came from. In these ways, each pear is unique, like us. Lastly, pear seeds could take a decade or more to produce fruit, so you might say that pears have to be patient, a lesson some of us are still trying to learn.

Over the centuries, botanists have developed ways to help pears grow faster and more predictably. Many gardeners graft pear trees, which means they cut a root from one plant and join it with the stem or leaves of another. This way, they know exactly what kind of pears they'll get, and can often begin harvesting fruit within a few years. Today, almost all pear trees are grown from grafted parts, but some of those parts are germinated (grown) from seed. For this book, illustrations would have been pretty difficult if the characters were a rootstock and branches (especially if they were being cut . . .) so I chose to make them seeds.

I could go on about the amazing things I've learned about nature and plant life cycles, but a good actor knows when to exit. So I'll take a bow and turn the spotlight on you— what will you discover next about pears, nature, or even yourself?

—Miranda Paul

5 "PEARY" SMART FACTS

- In China, people have been farming pears for thousands of years, and Ancient Greeks and Romans wrote about early grafting methods more than two thousand years ago.

- Pears belong to the scientific family *Rosaceae*, which means their "cousins" include apples, strawberries, almonds, and even roses.

- Not all pears are pear-shaped—nashi pears (also called Asian pears and other names), have a rounder, neckless shape.

- Today, many kinds of pear seeds are stored in cold vaults at USDA's National Seed Storage Laboratory in Ft. Collins, Colorado.

- The pear is the fifth most widely produced fruit in the world.

CREDITS
(also known as a bibliography)

Crassweller, Robert. "Growing New Fruit Tree Plants from Seed (Home Lawn and Garden)." Home Lawn and Garden (Penn State Extension), Penn State Extension, 2016. extension.psu.edu/plants/gardening/fact-sheets/home-orchard-production/growing-new-fruit-tree-plants-from-seed

Savonen, Carol. "Where Did Pears Come from?" Gardening, Oregon State University Extension, February 19, 2003. extension.oregonstate.edu/gardening/where-did-pears-come

Silva, G.J. et al. "Origin, Domestication, and Dispersing of Pear (*Pyrus* spp.)." *Advances in Agriculture*, vol. 2014, June 9, 2014, pp. 1–8. doi:10.1155/2014/541097

USApears.org. "Tree to Table." USA Pears, Pear Bureau Northwest, December 7, 2015. usapears.org/tree-to-table/